ISBN 0 86112 981 4
© Brimax Books 1995. All rights reserved.
Published by Brimax Books, Newmarket,
England CB8 7AU 1995.
Printed in Spain

OLIVER TWIST

ADAPTED BY
JOHN ESCOTT

ILLUSTRATED BY
ERIC KINCAID

Brimax . Newmarket . England

Introduction

Fagin, the Artful Dodger, Mr Bumble the beadle and young Oliver Twist himself ... just four of the characters from Charles Dickens' celebrated story of the workhouse orphan who dared to say "Please, sir, I want some more."

Oliver Twist is the story of a boy who is orphaned as a baby and cruelly brought up in the workhouse. At the age of nine he runs away to London, where he falls into the hands of the villainous Fagin and his gang. Terrified by the brutal Sikes, and befriended by Nancy and the roguish Dodger, Oliver seems doomed to a life of crime in the darkest haunts of Victorian London. Two strangers come into his life and they hold the key to his true identity and future.

Oliver Twist takes the reader back on a historical journey to a London of narrow, bustling lanes, noisy inns and the dark haunts of criminals. By day the streets are full of well-to-do ladies and gentlemen, street traders and crafty pickpockets. But at night as the ghostly fog creeps up the River Thames, London becomes a place where only scoundrels like Fagin and Sikes dare venture out.

This edition of Oliver Twist has been carefully abridged to make the text, which was originally written in serial form for a newspaper, the more accessible to young readers.

Contents

Chapter One

When Oliver Twist arrived in this world, he was not expected to live more than a few minutes. He was born in a workhouse, where the poor and homeless lived. Two people watched him struggle for his life; one was the surgeon, the other an old nurse.

Oliver gave his first cry, and the pale face of his young mother was raised from the pillow. "Let me see my child, and die," she said in a faint voice. She stretched out her hand and the baby was put into her arms. She hugged her son to her ... then sank back and died.

The surgeon got ready to leave. "The child is weak and will be probably be troublesome. Give it a little gruel if it is." He put on his hat and looked at the mother. "A good looking girl. Where did she come from?"

"She was found in the street, outside the workhouse," replied the old nurse. "Nobody knows where she came from, or where she was going."

Oliver was wrapped in a blanket. Looking at him, he could have been the son of a nobleman or of a beggar, but it no longer mattered. Now he was a child of the workhouse and doomed to a life of misery.

He was taken to the nursery and put into the care of a cruel old woman called Mrs Mann. But he had more spirit than most and the pale, thin child grew to the age of nine in spite of all he was forced to suffer.

He was spending his ninth birthday in the cellar for daring to be hungry when Mrs Mann saw Mr Bumble, the beadle, outside the gates. She hurried down to meet him. Mr Bumble always made her nervous. He was responsible for the poor people of the town, but did not like children.

They went into a small parlour and the beadle put his hat and cane on the table. "Oliver Twist is nine years old today," he said.

"Bless him," said Mrs Mann. "Tell me, how did he get his name?"

"I invented it," said Mr Bumble, proudly. Then went on to explain. "I follow the alphabet when choosing a name. The last orphan was an S, and I called him Swubble. This was a T, so I named him Twist. But it's time for Oliver to come back to the workhouse and earn his living."

So, with his little cap on his head and a slice of bread in his hand, Oliver was led away from that wretched home.

"You're going to be educated and taught a useful trade," said Mr Bumble. "Tomorrow you'll be put to work making string from old rope. You'll start at six o'clock."

That night Oliver sobbed himself to sleep.

The room in which the boys were fed was a large stone hall with a long bare table. At one end stood a copper pot where the master served one ladle of gruel to each boy. The

bowls never needed washing. The boys polished them with their spoons until they shone, then sucked their fingers and stared hungrily at the copper pot.

After three months of this slow starvation, one of Oliver's companions hinted that he'd soon eat the boy who slept next to him if he didn't get more food. Someone would have to ask the master for more food at suppertime, it was decided, and the task fell to Oliver. The evening arrived. The boys took their places and the gruel was served in the usual manner. After it had quickly disappeared, the other boys nudged and winked at little Oliver. He rose from the table and walked unsteadily towards the master, his empty bowl shaking in his hand. Then he spoke.

"Please sir, I want some more."

A terrible silence descended on the room.

The master's red face turned pale as he stared in astonishment at the small boy in front of him.

"What!" he said, faintly.

"Please sir," replied Oliver. "I want some more."

The master aimed a blow at Oliver's head with the ladle and screamed for the beadle. Mr Bumble came quickly and heard the dreadful news.

"He asked for *more*?" said Mr Bumble.

Oliver was taken to a dark room and locked inside. The next day, a notice was pasted outside the workhouse gates. It offered five pounds to any man or woman who would take Oliver off their hands and put him to work.

"That boy will hang one day!" said the master.

Oliver was kept in his dark prison for a week. Nobody seemed interested in Mr Bumble's offer of five pounds to take Oliver away. Mr Bumble began to consider the possibility of sending the boy away to sea. Then one day, Mr Sowerberry the local undertaker arrived at the workhouse.

Mr Bumble pointed to the notice on the gate. "Do you know of anyone who wants a boy, Mr Sowerberry?" He tapped his cane against the words Five Pounds to draw attention to the generosity of his offer.

Mr Sowerberry was thoughtful for a moment. "I could take the boy off your hands," he said eventually.

So Oliver was taken to the undertaker's house that evening. He carried everything he owned in a small brown paper parcel.

"If you complain about your work," Mr Bumble told him, "you'll be sent to sea and drowned. Do you understand?"

Tears slid down Oliver's cheeks as he was led through the street, and even Mr Bumble felt a twinge of pity. He coughed to cover his embarrassment, then told Oliver to dry his eyes and be a good boy.

Mr Sowerberry had just closed his shop when he arrived. He and his wife came to see the boy.

"He's very small," said Mrs Sowerberry.

"There's no denying that," agreed Mr Bumble. "But he'll grow."

The woman sniffed. "I dare say he will. But it will be us that will be feeding him! Get downstairs to the kitchen, boy!"

The dog had left some of its dinner, and it was this that Oliver was given to eat. Even so, he gobbled it down hungrily.

He slept amongst the shadows of the shop, half expecting to see some terrible shape rise up from the unfinished coffin that stood in the middle of the room; fearful that some cold, ghostly hand would touch him as he slept. Never before had Oliver felt so alone.

He was awakened in the morning by a loud kicking at the shop door.

"Open up, will yer?" cried a voice through the keyhole.

Oliver opened the door. "Did you want a coffin, sir?" he asked, seeing a large, fierce-looking boy.

"You'll be needin' one before long, work'us brat," said the boy. He had a large head and very small eyes. He kicked Oliver as he entered the shop. "I'm Noah Claypole, and you'll be working under me."

Later, Charlotte the housemaid gave them both breakfast. "Come near the fire, Noah," she said. "I've saved a nice bit of bacon for you. Oliver, take those bits on the bread pan."

They watched scornfully as Oliver took the scraps of food to a draughty corner of the room, shivering as he ate them.

Oliver's sad face made him highly suitable for leading funeral processions. A few weeks after his arrival, he was given a black hat and black stick and the job of walking ahead of the coffins.

But Noah Claypole quickly made Oliver's life unbearable.

"How's your mother, Work'us?" he said, a cruel gleam in his eye.

"She's dead," Oliver told him. "And don't say anything about her."

"What did she die of, Work'us?"

"A broken heart, so an old nurse told me," said Oliver sadly.

"It's as well she died when she did," jeered Noah. "She'd be in prison or hung by now. A right bad 'un, she was, Work'us."

Oliver seized Noah and shook him until the young man's teeth rattled.

"He'll murder me!" wailed Noah. "Help! Oliver's gone mad!"

Charlotte and Mrs Sowerberry ran into the room and pulled Oliver off Noah. Then they dragged him down to the cellar and locked the door. Noah ran to fetch Mr Bumble from the workhouse.

"Oliver's gone mad!" Noah told the beadle. "He tried to murder me, then he tried to murder Charlotte and Mrs Sowerberry!"

The two of them hurried back to the undertaker's shop where Oliver was kicking wildly at the cellar door.

"Oliver!" shouted Mr Bumble. "Do you know my voice? Aren't you trembling as I speak?"

"Let me out!" screamed Oliver. "I'm not afraid of you!"

Mr Bumble staggered back in astonishment. He looked at the others.

"He's mad," said Mrs Sowerberry. "No boy in his right mind would speak to you like that, Mr Bumble."

"It's not madness, Mrs Sowerberry," said Mr Bumble. "It's meat. You've over-fed him. If you'd kept him on gruel, ma'am, this would never have happened."

"I was too generous," sighed Mrs Sowerberry.

At this moment Mr Sowerberry arrived back and was told by his wife what had happened. He dragged Oliver from the cellar.

"Noah called my mother names," Oliver tried to explain.

"What if he did?" said Mr Sowerberry. "She deserved it, and worse."

"It's a lie," said Oliver.

Hearing this, Mrs Sowerberry burst into tears, and Mr Sowerberry felt obliged to beat Oliver. This was followed by another beating, this time from Mr Bumble, and then Oliver was sent to bed.

Alone in the coffin shop, Oliver cried bitter, lonely tears. The candle was burning low when he finally got to his feet, quietly opened the door and looked out into the cold, dark night. The stars seemed far away and the trees threw ghostly shadows on the ground. Oliver closed the door again and, in the dying light of the candle, bundled the few clothes he owned into a handkerchief and waited for morning.

At first light, Oliver slipped out into the streets.

Chapter Two

All that morning, Oliver ran and hid behind hedges, frightened that someone might be after him. When he had gone five miles, he sat down on a milestone to rest. The stone told him it was seventy miles to London.

'London,' thought Oliver. 'Not even Mr Bumble could find me there.'

That day he walked twenty miles, eating a dry crust of bread which he'd brought with him and begging for water at some cottages on the road. When night came, a cold and hungry Oliver slept in a haystack.

After seven days of walking and begging for food and water, Oliver arrived at the little town of Barnet, a few miles from the city. It was early and the town was just coming to life.

He had been sitting on a doorstep, resting and watching the passing coaches, when he noticed a boy on the opposite side of the road.

"Hallo, my young covey," said the boy, walking across to Oliver. "What's the matter?"

He was about Oliver's age, with a snub nose and sharp eyes. His hat was stuck on his head so lightly that it looked as though it would come off in a breeze, and he wore a man's coat which reached nearly to his heels.

"I'm tired and hungry," said Oliver. "I've walked for seven days."

"Going to London?" said the strange boy. "I suppose you'll want a place to sleep. Well, don't worry, I've got to be in London tonight and I know a respectable old gentleman who'll give you lodgings for nothing. I'm Jack Dawkins, known to my friends as the Artful Dodger."

It was after eleven o'clock when Oliver and his new friend arrived at Saffron Hill, a dirty, wretched place in the city. The Dodger pushed open a door and pulled Oliver into a dark passage.

"Who's that?" cried a voice.

"Plummy and slam!" replied the Dodger.

This seemed to be some kind of signal or password, for a candle gleamed at the end of the passage and a man's face appeared out of the shadows. "There's two of you," he said. "Who's the other one?"

"A new pal," said the Dodger.

They climbed some broken stairs into a dark and dirty back room. A candle stood in the centre of a table. Seated around it were five boys, smoking clay pipes and drinking beer like middle-aged men. A frying pan was on the fire and

an old man, his ugly face partly covered by a tangle of red beard, stood over it. He seemed to be dividing his attention between the frying pan and a number of silk handkerchiefs drying by the fire.

"This, Fagin," said the Dodger, "is my new friend, Oliver Twist."

The other boys came to shake Oliver's hand, while the old man bowed and said, "We're glad to see you, Oliver, my dear. I see you're looking at the handkerchiefs. There are a good many of them, aren't there? We've just got 'em out ready to wash, that's all. Ha, ha!"

The others joined in the laughter, then they began their supper. Fagin mixed a glass of gin and water for Oliver, telling him to drink it quickly, which Oliver did. Soon after, the boy felt himself being lifted on to some sacks, where he fell into a deep sleep.

It was late next morning when Oliver began to wake up. With half-closed eyes, he saw that Fagin was the only other person in the room. The old man was boiling coffee in a saucepan, but a moment or two later he came across to Oliver. Thinking the boy was still asleep, he locked the door and took a small box from a secret hole in the floor. He put the box on the table and sat down.

Muttering to himself, Fagin removed a gold watch from the box. He smiled at it, then began to take out other valuables – rings, brooches, bracelets, and several more gold watches. At that moment, he looked up and saw Oliver's eyes on him. Fagin slammed the box shut and picked up the bread knife that was on the table.

"Why do you watch me, boy?" he said, his eyes blazing with anger. "What have you seen? Speak, boy! Quick–quick, for your life!"

"I wasn't able to sleep any longer, sir," replied Oliver, meekly.

"You weren't awake an hour ago?" said Fagin, scowling.

"No. No, indeed, sir!"

The scowl disappeared and the voice became softer.

"Did you see any of these pretty things, my dear?" Fagin touched the little box.

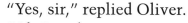

"Yes, sir," replied Oliver.

"Ah," said Fagin, turning rather pale. "They – they're mine, Oliver. My little property. All I have to live on in my old age. Folks call me a miser, my dear. Only a miser, that's all."

Oliver got up and washed himself. Soon after, the Dodger and another of the boys – Charley Bates – returned. Fagin glanced at Oliver but spoke to the Dodger. "Have you been at work this morning, my dears?"

"Hard at work," replied the Dodger.

"And what have you got?"

"A couple of wallets," answered the Dodger.

Fagin carefully looked at the insides. "Not so heavy as they might be, but very neat and nicely made. A good workman, isn't he, Oliver?"

"Very good, sir," agreed Oliver, which made Charley Bates laugh.

"And what have you got, my dear?" Fagin asked Charley.

"Handkerchiefs," the other boy replied, and gave him four.

Fagin examined them. "They're good ones," he said.

"Wouldn't you like to be able to make handkerchiefs as easily as Charley, Oliver?"

"Very much, sir," said Oliver, "if you'll teach me."

Charley laughed again, almost choking.

After breakfast, Fagin and the two boys played a very curious game. The old man placed a snuff-box in one trouser pocket, a wallet in the other, a watch in his waistcoat, and a handkerchief in his coat pocket. Then he trotted up and down the room with a stick, like an old gentleman walking the streets. The two boys followed him closely, hiding quickly whenever the old man turned round. Then the Dodger stepped on Fagin's toes and Charley stumbled against him. In that one moment, with the speed of lightning, they took the snuff-box, wallet, watch and handkerchief off him.

The game was played over and over again, and if Fagin felt a hand in any of his pockets, he cried out and it began once more. Later, two young ladies arrived. One was called Bet, the other Nancy. They had untidy hair and heavily painted faces, but they were friendly, and Oliver liked them. Then Charley said it was time to go out, and the four of them left.

Oliver was left alone with Fagin.

"Is my handkerchief hanging out of my pocket?" the old man asked him.

"Yes, sir," said Oliver.

"See if you can take it without my feeling it."

Oliver held the bottom of the pocket with one hand, as he had seen the Dodger do it, then lightly pulled the handkerchief from it with the other.

"Is it gone?" cried Fagin.

"Here it is, sir," said Oliver, showing it in his hand.

"You're a clever boy, my dear," said the playful old gentleman, patting Oliver on the head. "Here's a shilling for you. If you go on this way, you'll be the greatest man of all time."

Oliver wondered how picking the old man's pocket could improve his chances of becoming a great man, but he said nothing.

Chapter Three

For many days, Oliver remained in Fagin's rooms, playing the same strange game every morning. The Dodger and Charley Bates went out to work each day, but sometimes came home empty-handed. When they did, Fagin became very angry, often sending the boys to bed without any supper.

Then came the morning when Oliver was allowed to go out with the other boys. Off they went, the Dodger with his coat sleeves tucked up and Charley with his hands in his pockets. Suddenly, the Dodger stopped.

"Do you see that old gent at the bookstall?" he whispered.

"Yes, I see him," said Oliver.

"He'll do."

Oliver watched in silent amazement as Charley and the Dodger walked up behind the old gentleman – a very respectable-looking person with gold spectacles. He was reading something at the bookstall.

Oliver, his eyes wide with horror, saw the Dodger plunge his hand into the old man's pocket and draw out a handkerchief. He gave it to Charley, and the two of them ran away round the corner at full speed.

That instant, the whole mystery of the handkerchiefs, the jewellery and Fagin became clear, and a terrified Oliver stood with the blood tingling through his veins. Then he ran, like a frightened hare.

At the same time, the old gentlemen put a hand into his pocket and found that his handkerchief had gone. Seeing Oliver running away, he naturally assumed the boy to be the thief.

"Stop, thief!" he shouted, and ran after Oliver.

The Dodger and Charley had stopped round the first corner, and they heard the old man shout. Like good citizens, they too shouted, "Stop, thief!" and joined the old gentleman and the many street traders and shoppers who were taking part in the chase.

Away they ran, helter-skelter and slap-dash, yelling and screaming, "Stop, thief! Stop, thief!" until Oliver was brought down on the pavement, covered in mud and dust, and bleeding from his mouth.

"Is this the boy?" somebody asked the old gentlemen.

"Yes," he said, "I am afraid it is. Poor fellow, he's hurt himself."

A policeman was making his way through the crowd. He seized Oliver by the collar. "Get up!" he said, roughly.

"It wasn't me, sir," cried Oliver, looking around. "It was two other boys. They're here somewhere."

But the Dodger and Charley were nowhere to be seen.

"Don't hurt him," said the old man, looking distressed.

"Oh, I won't hurt him!" said the policeman, tearing Oliver's jacket half off his back. "Stand on your legs, you young devil!"

Oliver was dragged along the street by his jacket collar.

The old man went with them.

Oliver was taken to the police station and locked in a small stone cell. The old gentleman looked most unhappy.

"There is something in that boy's face," he said to himself. "Where have I seen someone like him before?"

Later, he was taken to see the magistrate, Mr Fang, a lean, stiff-necked man who was almost bald. He scowled at the old gentleman.

"Who are you?" he said.

"My name, sir, is Brownlow," said the old gentleman.

"What's this man charged with, officer?" Mr Fang asked the policeman.

"He's not charged with anything," replied the police officer. "He's accusing the boy of picking his pocket."

"I was standing at the bookstall – " began Mr Brownlow.

"Hold your tongue!" said Mr Fang.

"I will not, sir!" replied Mr Brownlow. "I am not sure now that this boy took my handkerchief. I saw him running away but – "

"Hold your tongue!" said the magistrate.

Oliver was deadly pale. The room seemed to be spinning round him.

"Can I have some water?" he gasped.

"I think the boy is ill, your worship," said the policeman.

And at that moment, Oliver fell to the floor in a dead faint.

"Let him lie there," said Mr Fang. "He'll soon be tired of that. The boy is sentenced to three months in prison."

Suddenly, a man rushed into the room. An angry Mr Fang turned on him. "What's this?" he said. "Turn this man out! Clear the room!"

"But I saw it all," said the man. "It was my bookstall. Another boy took the gentleman's handkerchief." He went on to tell how he saw the Dodger and Charley pick the pocket and run away.

Mr Fang turned to the policeman. "Let the boy go free," he said. "It seems that he's innocent."

Oliver was carried from the court.

"Poor boy, poor boy!" said Mr Brownlow. "Call a coach, someone."

A coach was called and Mr Brownlow lifted Oliver on to a seat, then the coach drove the two of them away.

It stopped at a neat house in a quiet, shady street near Pentonville. Here a bed was found for Oliver, and he was looked after with love and kindness. But for many days, whilst he suffered from a fever, he was unaware of this.

Weak and pale, he at last awoke from what seemed to have been a long and troubled dream. "Where am I?" he asked.

"Hush, my dear," said Mrs Bedwin, Mr Brownlow's kindly old housekeeper. "You must be very quiet, or you'll be ill again."

After several more days, Oliver was well enough to be carried down to Mrs Bedwin's room. She sat him by the fireside, then made him some soup. As he ate it, he found himself looking at a portrait of a lady hanging on the wall.

"What a beautiful face," he said. "Who is it?"

"I don't know, my dear," said Mrs Bedwin. "I don't expect it's anyone you or I know."

There was a sudden knock at the door, then in came Mr Brownlow.

"How do you feel?" he asked Oliver.

"Very happy," replied Oliver. "And very grateful for your kindness to me, sir."

"Good boy," said Mr Brownlow. "Now what is your full name?"

"Oliver Twist, sir. I hope you're not angry with me."

"No, not in the least ..." Mr Brownlow was staring at the portrait. "Look, Bedwin!" He pointed to the picture and then to the boy's face. It was a living copy; the eyes, the mouth – every feature was the same.

After Charley Bates and the Dodger had left the crowd chasing Oliver, they made their way back to Fagin's house.

"Where's Oliver?" Fagin wanted to know. Neither boy answered, and Fagin grabbed the Dodger's collar. "Speak up, or I'll throttle you!"

"The police have him," said the Dodger, sullenly. "Let me go, will you?" And he slipped out of the coat, leaving it empty in Fagin's hands.

Fagin picked up a pot and threw it at the Dodger, but the boy ducked out of the way. At that very moment, the door opened and the pot narrowly missed the man entering the room.

"What the blazes is going on?" he growled. He was a man of about thirty-five, wearing a black coat, dirty trousers, a brown hat, and a dirty handkerchief around his neck. His chin had a three-day growth of beard on it, and one of his eyes had been blackened in a recent fight. A white dog, with its face torn and scratched, skulked in behind him. The man kicked the dog into the corner of the room, ordering it to lie down.

He turned to the two boys. "What's happened?" he asked them.

The Dodger told him how Oliver had been caught by the police.

"I'm afraid, Mr Sikes," said Fagin, "that the boy will say something that will get us into trouble."

"Very likely," said Bill Sikes, with an evil grin. "The game's up for you, Fagin."

"And if it's up for us, it might be up for a good many others," said Fagin. "You might come out of it rather worse than me, my dear."

The grin slipped from Sikes' face. "We must find out what happened at the magistrate's office. The boy must be found and brought back!"

But none of them wanted to go anywhere near a police station.

The problem was solved by the arrival of the two ladies, Nancy and Bet. Nancy was Bill Sikes' girl, and she did whatever he told her. She was too afraid of him to do otherwise.

She was sent to the court-house where she pretended to be Oliver's sister and told them that he had run away from home. She discovered how Oliver had been released from

the court, and taken away in a coach by Mr Brownlow. She spoke to a man who had overheard Mr Brownlow give a coach driver instructions to drive to somewhere in Pentonville.

She took the news back to Fagin's house. As soon as Bill Sikes heard it, he quickly called his white dog, put on his hat, and left them.

"We must know where Oliver is," Fagin told the Dodger and Charley. "We must find him and kidnap him! Now, go and skulk about the streets until you have some news of him. Nancy, you must help too. Oliver must be found!"

Chapter Four

Oliver slowly began to recover his strength. Everyone in Mr Brownlow's house treated him with great kindness, and no longer thought that he was a thief or a bad boy in any way. But Mr Brownlow had a friend, Mr Grimwig, who was less certain about Oliver's honesty. He was with Mr Brownlow when the old gentleman wanted to return some books to a bookseller, and to settle an outstanding bill.

"Send Oliver," suggested Mr Grimwig, with a smile.

Mr Brownlow hesitated, but he did not like the way the other man thought Oliver was not to be trusted. "Very well," he said.

So that evening, Oliver was sent out with the books under his arm and a five-pound note in his pocket.

"I won't be ten minutes," he said, pleased to be of some help.

Mrs Bedwin watched him go. "I can't bear to let him out of my sight, even for a little while," she sighed.

"You really expect him to come back?" said Mr Grimwig.

"He has new clothes, a five-pound note and some valuable books. He'll go straight to his thieving friends. If that boy comes back, I'll eat my hat!"

Oliver was walking to the bookshop when he took a wrong turning. Suddenly, he was startled by a young woman screaming, "Oh, my dear brother!" and hardly had time to look up when a pair of arms were thrown tightly round his neck.

"Let me go!" cried Oliver.

The young woman took no notice.

"What's the matter?" asked an onlooker.

"He ran away from home a month ago and joined a gang of thieves," the young woman said. "It almost broke his mother's heart."

"It's not true!" shouted Oliver. But nobody believed him. Then he saw the young woman's face. "It's Nancy!" he cried.

"You see?" said Nancy, triumphantly. "He knows me!"

Bill Sikes and his white dog burst out of a nearby public house. "What's this? Young Oliver! Come home to your poor Mother! Here, Bulls-eye. Mind the boy!"

Weak from his recent illness and terrified by the fierce dog, Oliver was powerless. In another minute, he was being dragged through the maze of dirty streets and alleyways. "Help! Help!" he cried.

But his cries went unheard.

Oliver and his captors were crossing Smithfield Market. It was dark and foggy, the lights in the shops were barely able to penetrate the gloom. A church bell struck eight o'clock as they hurried through the murky night.

The Dodger led them into Fagin's house. Charley Bates whooped with laughter when he saw Oliver dressed so nicely.

"Delighted to see you looking so well, my dear," said Fagin, with a little bow. "The Dodger will get you another suit. We don't want you spoiling your Sunday best ..."

The Dodger smiled. His nimble fingers had already lifted the five-pound note from Oliver's pocket. But Sikes snatched the money from his grasp before Fagin could lay his hands on it.

"That's for Nancy and me," he told Fagin, "for our trouble. You can keep the books, if you're fond of reading. If not sell 'em."

"They belong to the old gentleman," cried Oliver.

"Please send back the books and the money, or he'll think I stole them."

A cruel smile spread slowly across Fagin's face. "You're right, Oliver. He *will* think you stole them. Ha! Ha! How splendid!" Oliver jumped to his feet and tore wildly from the room, his cries for help echoing through the whole building. Fagin, Charley and the Dodger darted out after him, but Nancy darted in front of Sikes and his dog.

"Keep the dog back," she pleaded. "He'll tear the boy to pieces!"

"Get out of my way," snarled Sikes. And he threw the girl across the room just as Fagin and the two boys returned, dragging Oliver between them.

"What's the matter here?" asked Fagin.

"The girl's gone mad," replied Sikes.

Fagin turned to Oliver. "So you wanted to get away, did you? Wanted to go to the police, eh?" He took a lump of wood from the fireplace and hit Oliver across the shoulders with it.

Nancy snatched the wood from Fagin's hand and threw it into the fire. "You've got the boy, what more do you want, Fagin? You'll turn him into a liar and a thief, isn't that enough? It's what you did to me when I was half Oliver's age, and now look at me! The cold, wet, dirty streets are my home, and you're the wretch who drove me to them and who'll keep me there until the day I die!" Nancy's rage boiled over and she made a dive at Fagin, but Sikes caught her wrists just in time to save the old man. She struggled for a moment, then fainted.

Fagin wiped his forehead. "Charley, put Oliver to bed," he said.

Oliver was taken to a dark room where he was locked in. Sick and weary, he soon fell fast asleep.

Chapter Five

A few days later, at a public house near to the place Oliver was being kept prisoner, a large fat beadle took his glass of wine and drew his chair nearer to the fire. Then he began to read his newspaper. Mr Bumble's eyes rested on an advertisement:

> Five guineas reward will be paid to
> any person with information about a boy
> called Oliver Twist who ran away, or was
> kidnapped, from his home in Pentonville
> last Thursday evening.

Beneath this was a description of Oliver, together with Mr Brownlow's name and address.

An astonished Mr Bumble read the words several times, and in less than five minutes was on his way to Pentonville.

Mrs Bedwin greeted him at the door of Mr Brownlow's house.

"I have information about Oliver Twist," said Mr Bumble.

He was quickly taken to Mr Brownlow's study where the old gentleman and his friend Mr Grimwig were sitting.

"Do you know where the boy is now?" asked Mr Brownlow.

Mr Bumble shook his head. "No, I am afraid not."

"Well, what do you know of him?"

Mr Bumble put down his hat and unbuttoned his coat. He told how Oliver was born and had lived comfortably at the workhouse, and how the ungrateful child had attacked a boy at his place of employment, and had then run away from his master. The old gentleman listened sadly.

"I fear it's all too true," he said.

"I don't believe it!" said Mrs Bedwin. "Oliver was a gentle child."

"I knew it all along," said Mr Grimwig. "The boy was no good."

"Never let me hear that boy's name again," said Mr Brownlow.

"How ungrateful of you to run away from us, my dear," Fagin told Oliver the next day. "Us, your friends, who took you in when you were homeless and hungry! There was once another boy who went to the police with stories about his friends ... but he was hanged before he had the chance to tell them." Fagin placed a bony hand round Oliver's throat. "You don't want to hang, do you, my dear?"

Oliver's blood ran cold.

Fagin patted him on the head and smiled his twisted smile. "Be a good boy and do as I tell you," he said, "and we can still be friends." Then taking his hat and coat, he went out, locking the door behind him.

And so Oliver remained for all that day, and for several days after, eating and sleeping alone. He thought a lot about Mr Brownlow and the kindly Mrs Bedwin, and wondered miserably what they thought of him now.

One cold, windy night, Fagin went out to see Bill Sikes and Nancy. He slipped in and out of the shadows of the narrow streets until he came to one lit by a single lamp. Here he knocked on a door, muttered a few words to the person who opened it, then went upstairs.

A dog growled as he touched the handle of a door at the top.

"Who's there?" came the voice of Bill Sikes.

"Only me, Bill, my dear," answered Fagin, stepping inside.

Bill Sikes and Nancy were sitting close to the fire and Fagin went to join them, warming his hands over the flames.

"What brings you here, Fagin?" said Sikes.

"The robbery at Chertsey, Bill," said Fagin. "You know what I mean, my dear? He knows what I mean, don't he, Nancy?" Fagin rubbed his hands together. "When's it to be done, Bill?"

"Never," replied Sikes. "Unless you can find me a boy.

The place is barred like a prison, except in one place."

Fagin thought for a moment, then signalled to Sikes that he wanted Nancy out of the room.

"She won't talk," Sikes told him. "Will you Nancy?"

"No," said Nancy. She laughed. "Tell Bill about Oliver, Fagin!"

"You're a clever one," smiled Fagin. "It was Oliver I was going to suggest. I've had my eye on him. Once he's done a job, once he feels he's one of us, we'll have him! He'll be ours for life!"

"When is it to be done?" asked Nancy.

"Tomorrow night," said Sikes.

It was agreed that Nancy should come for Oliver the next evening.

The next night, when Nancy came for Oliver, her face was pale.

"Are you alright?" Oliver asked her.

"God forgive me!" she cried. "I never thought I would do this."

"What is it?" he said.

"I've come from Bill Sikes," she said. "You have to come with me."

"What for?" asked Oliver, suddenly afraid.

"You won't be harmed," said Nancy. "I've saved you once, and I'll save you again, Oliver, but tonight you must do as you're told. But remember, whatever they make you do, it's not your fault."

Sikes was waiting for them in his room.

"So you've got the boy," he said to Nancy. "Did he come quietly?"

"Like a lamb," said Nancy.

Sikes pulled a pistol from his pocket and put it against Oliver's forehead. "If you say one word when we're outside, except when I speak to you, I'll blow you're head off," he said. "Do you hear me?"

There was little sleep for Oliver that night. At half-past five, when it was barely light, Sikes said goodbye to Nancy and took Oliver out into the wet and windy morning. They crossed London on foot, the streets gradually filling with people as the morning wore on. They passed Hyde Park Corner, then Sikes saw an empty cart and asked the driver for a lift.

As the milestones and the hours slipped by and London was left behind, Oliver wondered where Sikes was taking him. They were out in the country, and a damp mist rose from the river and the marshy ground. Oliver sat huddled in a corner of the cart as the darkness closed in around him.

A church clock struck seven and, a few miles on, the cart stopped. Sikes and Oliver got down and began to walk again. After some time, they came to a bridge and Oliver saw the river running underneath.

'The water!' he thought, turning sick with fear. 'He's brought me here to this lonely place to murder me!'

But he saw they were near an old ruin of a house which seemed to be empty. Sikes approached the door and lifted the latch.

"Hallo!" cried a voice, as the two of them went inside.

"Don't make such a row," said Sikes, bolting the door behind him.

A man came out of the darkness, carrying a candle. "Bill, my boy! I'm glad to see you. I'd almost given you up." He suddenly saw Oliver.

"Who's this?" he demanded.

"It's only the boy," replied Sikes, following the other man into a room. He drew up a chair near the fire. "Get us some food while we're waiting. Oliver, sit by the fire and rest, we're going out again later."

The other man, whose name was Toby Crackit, brought food which they ate beside the fire. Much later, after Oliver had dozed on and off, Crackit took a pair of pistols and a crowbar from a cupboard, and the three of them went out into the night.

It was now very dark and the fog much thicker than earlier. They crossed a bridge, then hurried through the main street of a little town. It was silent and deserted, and a church clock struck two o'clock.

A quarter of a mile on, they stopped in front of a house that was surrounded by a wall. Crackit climbed the wall quickly. "The boy next," he said, and Oliver found himself being pushed up by Sikes. In less than a minute, the three of them were on the other side.

And now, for the first time, Oliver realised in horror why they were here – *robbery, and perhaps even murder!* "Let me go!" he cried. "Don't make me steal!"

Sikes swore and took the pistol from his pocket, but Crackit knocked it from his grasp and put a hand over the boy's mouth. He dragged Oliver over to the house.

"Say another word and I'll kill you myself," he whispered.

Sikes, still cursing, used the crowbar to open a window at the back of the house. The opening was just big enough for a boy to get through.

"Now listen," Sikes whispered, taking a small lantern from his coat pocket and shining it in Oliver's face.

"I'm going to put you through here. Take this light, go up the steps and along the little hall to the front door. Unfasten it, and let us in."

Oliver, more dead than alive with fear, was lifted into the house. He had already decided what to do, even if he died in the attempt. He would dart up the stairs and warn the family.

A noise came from the hall.

"Come back!" cried Sikes. "Back! Back!"

A startled Oliver dropped the lantern, unable to move. Another light appeared, and he saw two half-dressed men at the top of the stairs. There was a flash – a loud noise – smoke – a crash! Oliver staggered back. Sikes reached in and caught hold of the boy's collar, firing his pistol at the two men. He dragged Oliver through the window.

"They've hit him!" shouted Sikes. "Look how he bleeds!"

A bell rang, mingling with the noise of more gunfire and the shouts of men. Sikes put Oliver over his shoulder and ran, Crackit ahead of him.

"Help me with the boy!" Sikes shouted, but Crackit kept running.

Sikes dropped Oliver on the ground. He threw a cape over the boy, then ran on, disappearing into the mist.

Chapter Six

The night was cold. Bleak, dark and piercing cold. Mr Bumble shook the snow off his clothes as he stood outside the workhouse where Oliver had been born. Mrs Corney, the matron, was opening the door.

"Hard weather, Mr Bumble," she said, taking him inside.

Mrs Corney gave him a cup of tea and was surprised to be rewarded with the warmest of smiles. The matron, who was a widow, found herself blushing. The two of them sat at the table and, little by little, Mr Bumble moved closer to her until their chairs touched. Her hand shook and her heart beat fast with excitement.

"What a kind person you are, Mrs Corney," said Mr Bumble. And he leaned across to give her a kiss.

"Mr Bumble!" the lady protested (but not too much). "I'll scream!"

Mr Bumble made no reply, but in a slow and dignified manner, put his arm round the matron's waist. However, at that moment a knock came at the door and he moved quickly away.

An old woman put her head around the door. "Old Sally is dying fast," she said, "but she says she has something to tell you."

Muttering angrily, then asking Mr Bumble to wait for her return, Mrs Corney snatched up a thick shawl and followed the woman.

Immediately, Mr Bumble began opening cupboards and drawers, counting the teaspoons and checking to see if the milk pot was made of real silver.

Old Sally lay dying in a bare room at the top of the house. She clutched the matron's arm. "Listen to me," she said, her voice weak. "In this very room – in this very bed – I nursed

a pretty young woman who was brought here. She gave birth to a boy and then died."

"What about her?" said Mrs Corney.

"I robbed her," said Sally. "She was hardly dead when I stole it."

"Stole what?"

"Gold! Rich gold that might have saved her life!"

"Gold?" echoed the matron. "Who was the mother? When was it?"

"She asked me to keep it safe," gasped the old woman.

"The boy grew so like his mother that I could never forget it when I saw his face."

"The boy's name!" demanded Mrs Corney. "Before it's too late!"

"They call him Oliver," replied Sally. "The gold I stole was ..."

"Yes, yes – what?" cried Mrs Corney.

But the old woman was dead.

A dirty scrap of paper fell from her hand.

Mr Bumble made a decision as he heard the matron returning.

"I'll do it!" he said to himself.

It was a breathless Mrs Corney who threw herself into a chair.

"What has upset you?" Mr Bumble asked.

"Nothing," replied the matron. "I'm a foolish, weak creature."

Mr Bumble comforted her with a kiss. "The master of the workhouse is dying," he said after a moment. "He's not expected to last a week."

"I know," Mrs Corney replied, trying to conceal her excitement at what she was sure the beadle was about to say next.

"And his death will cause a vacancy for a new master," went on Mr Bumble. "And a new ... mistress? Oh, Mrs Corney, what an opportunity! Can we be married? Say we can!"

Mrs Corney smiled blissfully. "Oh, yes!" she sighed.

At this moment, Toby Crackit was arriving at Fagin's house.

"Where's Bill?" screamed Fagin. "Where's Oliver?"

"We failed," Toby said, faintly. "They fired and hit the boy, and we ran away. Bill had the boy on his back, but we parted company and left the youngster in a ditch. I don't know if he's alive or dead."

Fagin did not wait to hear more. He let out a loud yell and rushed from the house. He avoided the main streets, skulking through dark alleyways until he reached the Three Cripples Inn. There he walked straight upstairs to a dimly-lit room and stepped inside, looking around.

A man came across. "What can I do for you, Mr Fagin?" he said.

"Is he here?" asked Fagin.

"Monks, do you mean?" the man said.

"Hush!" said Fagin, not wanting the name to be heard. "Yes."

"He'll be here in ten minutes. If you can wait – "

"No," said Fagin, hastily. "Tell him I was here and must see him."

After leaving the Three Cripples Inn, Fagin went to Bill Sikes' house where he found Nancy alone, her head on the table.

'She's been drinking,' Fagin thought.

She looked up. "Any news?" she asked.

Fagin told her Toby Crackit's story. "And where do you think Bill is now, my dear?" he asked her.

"I don't know," she said.

"And the boy?"

"He'll be better off than us if he's dead," she said.

Fagin became angry. "That boy's worth hundreds of pounds to me. If he fails to come back, I'll see Bill Sikes is hanged. Remember that!"

He left her slumped across the table and went out into the night.

It was almost midnight and a sharp wind whistled through the streets. Fagin reached his house and was fumbling in his pocket for the door key when a dark figure emerged from the shadows.

"Fagin!" whispered a voice close to his ear.

"Ah!" said Fagin. "Is that you, Monks?"

"Yes," said the other man. "Where have you been?"

"On your business, my dear," replied Fagin.

He opened the door and they both slipped inside. Then they talked in whispers, so as not to wake the boys upstairs. Monks was angry.

"It was badly planned," he said. "Why didn't you keep Oliver with you? You could have made him a pickpocket, had him arrested, and he'd have been sent out of the country, perhaps for life."

"It wasn't easy to make this boy into a thief," said Fagin. "Look what happened when I sent him out with the Dodger and Charley."

"That wasn't my doing."

"No, but if he hadn't been arrested, you'd never have clapped eyes on him and realised that he was the boy you were looking for," Fagin reminded him.

"I know that," agreed Monks.

"Then I got him back for you, with Nancy's help," said Fagin, "and now the girl feels sorry for him."

"Throttle her," said Monks.

"We can't afford to do that just now," said Fagin, smiling. "One day, perhaps. Now if the boy's alive, I'll make him into a thief, as you wish. But if he's dead ..."

"It's not my fault if he is!" cried Monks, a look of terror on his face. "If they shot him dead, it's nothing to do with me." He jumped. "What's that?"

"What?" said Fagin. "Where?"

"I saw a shadow on that wall!" he said, pointing to the wall opposite the door. "A woman in a cloak and bonnet!"

"It was your imagination," said Fagin.

"I swear I saw it," said Monks, trembling violently.

The two of them looked in every part of the house but found no sign of the mysterious woman.

Chapter Seven

When Sikes dropped Oliver in the ditch and ran away, he did not stop to look back. If he had, he would have realised that the two men from the house had soon given up the chase. Both had thought it too dangerous to carry on once they were out in the foggy darkness of the open countryside.

When morning came, Oliver continued to lay motionless in the ditch. The air grew colder and rain began to fall. At last he stirred, the pain in his blood-soaked arm jarred him awake. He felt so weak he could hardly stand, but he knew if he stayed where he was he would die.

He staggered forward, his mind whirling with confused memories of what had happened. At last, he came to a road and saw a house ahead of him. Gathering up his strength, he moved towards it.

When he drew closer, Oliver realised it was the very same house they had attempted to rob the night before! But his strength was almost gone and he was left with no choice. He pushed open the gate and tottered across to the front door. After knocking at it faintly, Oliver sank to the ground.

Inside the house, the two men servants were telling the cook and the housemaid about their adventures. The women listened with admiration as Mr Giles described how he had shot at the robbers. All were enjoying themselves ... until that knock came at the door.

Nobody was keen to see who it was. Could the robbers have returned? Eventually, it was decided that they would all go to the door.

They found the exhausted Oliver slumped outside.

"A boy!" said Mr Giles. "He's one of them!"

The woman ran to tell their mistress as the men dragged Oliver in.

A doctor was called to tend Oliver's wounds.

"Can this poor child really be one of the robbers?" said Mrs Maylie, the owner of the house. She and her young niece, Rose, were looking at the sleeping Oliver as he lay against the pillows in a large bed.

"He's so young," agreed Rose, her eyes wet with tears. She was not yet seventeen, but had quite a beauty and a gentle nature. "My dear aunt, please remember this before you let them drag this child off to prison: I was once without a home, until you took me in and loved me like the mother I never knew."

"My dear love," said Mrs Maylie, putting her arms around the weeping girl, "do you think I would harm a hair of his head? But Giles is already downstairs with the police constables."

The doctor looked thoughtful. "I have a plan," he said, and explained it to Mrs Maylie and her niece.

Downstairs, Mr Giles and the other servant, Mr Brittles, were boasting about their adventures to the policemen. The men were drinking their third glass of beer when the doctor came into the kitchen.

"How is the patient?" asked Mr Giles.

"He's just awake, and telling the two ladies his sad story," replied the doctor, looking very serious. "Now, Giles, can you be sure the boy upstairs is the one who broke into the house?"

The doctor sounded so angry that Mr Giles and Mr Brittles became nervous and confused. Suddenly, they found it difficult to speak.

"A house is broken into, constable," went on the doctor, before they could find their tongues, "and a couple of men catch one moment's glimpse of a boy in the half-darkness, in the midst of a lot of gun-smoke and noise. Then a boy comes to the same house the next morning, and because he has an injured arm, the two men drag him inside – so putting his life in danger, mind you! – and swear he's the thief!"

"But the boy's injury – " began one policeman.

"The result of a prank," said the doctor. "The boy was accidentally shot whilst on Mr Whatsit's land at the back of here. He came here for assistance. Now have another glass of beer, constable, and let's think again about this whole business ..."

By the time the police constables left, some hours and

several beers later, they were quite certain Oliver was not the boy they were after.

Over several weeks, Oliver recovered from his injuries in the kind care of Mrs Maylie and Rose. He was very happy there, but one thing caused him sadness. He wanted to find Mr Brownlow and Mrs Bedwin who had been so good to him. But when Oliver was well enough to be taken to London, they found Mr Brownlow's house empty.

"He's sold up and moved to the West Indies," a neighbour told them.

This was a bitter disappointment to Oliver, who wanted to clear his name with the old gentleman, but he was more than happy to go on living with Mrs Maylie and Rose. They gave him lessons and took him for walks in the fields and woods. His nightmares of Fagin and Sikes soon faded away.

It was summer when Rose became ill with the fever. Oliver was sent to fetch Dr Losberne. He ran across the fields and along the lanes, hardly stopping for breath until he reached the town.

He was passing an inn when a tall man wrapped in a cloak came out of the door and Oliver stumbled into him. It was Mr Monks.

"I beg your pardon, sir," said Oliver. "I didn't see you coming."

Monks stared at the boy with his dark eyes. "Who would have thought it!" he exclaimed. He shook his fist at Oliver. "Rot your bones! Curses upon your head and black death upon your heart, you imp! What are you doing here?" He moved towards the boy, as if to hit him, but suddenly collapsed on the ground in a violent fit.

Oliver hurried to fetch help, certain that the man was mad, then ran on quickly to make up for lost time.

Dr Losberne did what he could for Rose but she grew much worse and everyone was afraid she would die. It was during this time that Oliver learned Rose was not Mrs Maylie's niece but an orphan, just like himself.

"She never knew her mother either," Mrs Maylie told him.

They prayed for Rose's recovery and, one morning, Dr Losberne brought the news they had all been waiting for.

"The fever has passed," he said. "Now she'll get better."

Life became a happy time again for Oliver, and he worked hard at his lessons. One evening, he was sitting in the room which he used for his studies. It was a warm night and he had been working so hard that he fell asleep in his chair. He began to dream.

Fagin appeared in his dreams, with another man.

"It's the boy," he thought he heard Fagin say. "We've found him."

"As if I could mistake him!" the other man seemed to answer. "If you buried him fifty feet down in an unmarked grave, I'd still know it was him under the ground!"

The man spoke with such hatred that Oliver woke up – *and found it wasn't a dream.* At the window – so close that he could have almost touched them – were Fagin and the man who had behaved so wildly outside the inn!

Oliver screamed, and the two men vanished immediately.

Although the servants searched the grounds afterwards, no sign of Fagin or the other man was found.

Chapter Eight

Mr Bumble had been married to Mrs Corney for two months, and was now master of the workhouse. But he was not a happy man. Life with his new bride seemed more like a prison sentence than a marriage, for she bullied and scolded him from morning until night.

One evening, in an effort to avoid her sharp tongue, Mr Bumble escaped to a nearby inn. A tall man was sitting at a table in the corner and he looked up at Mr Bumble.

"I've seen you before," he said. "Weren't you the beadle here?"

"I was," sighed Mr Bumble.

"That's lucky," said the other man. "I came here hoping to find you. I'm after some information, and I'll pay you for it." And he pushed two sovereigns across the table.

Mr Bumble looked at them to make sure they were genuine, then he put them in his waistcoat pocket.

"Now, think back – let me see – twelve years ago last winter," said the other man. "A certain boy was born at the workhouse."

"You mean Oliver Twist!" said Mr Bumble. "I remember him. There wasn't a more obstinate boy – "

"It's not him I want to hear about," interrupted the stranger. "It's the old woman who nursed his mother. Where is she?"

"She died last winter," replied Mr Bumble. But he sensed this was important and saw a way of earning more money. "My wife was with her when she was on her death-bed. Perhaps she can help."

"When can I see her?" asked the other man.

"Tomorrow," said Mr Bumble.

"At nine in the evening," said the stranger, writing an address on a scrap of paper. He stood up and gave it to Mr Bumble. "Bring her there."

"And your name?"

"Monks," whispered the stranger, and hurried out into the night.

The next evening found Mr Bumble and his wife outside a very large ruin of a mill near a river, in an area populated mostly by criminals. There was a sudden clap of thunder and it began to pour with rain.

A door opened and there was Monks. "Come in quickly," he said.

They followed him into the mill and Monks looked at Mrs Bumble. "So you were present when the old woman died, were you?"

"Yes," said Mrs Bumble. "And she told me something

about the mother of Oliver Twist. But what are you willing to pay me?"

"Twenty pounds, if it's what I want to hear," said Monks.

"Twenty-five pounds," said Mrs Bumble, "and I'll tell you all I know."

Monks hesitated for a moment, then took the money from his pocket and pushed it across the table. "Now let's hear your story," he said.

The heads of the three nearly touched as the two men leaned over the table to hear what the woman had to say. Thunder rumbled overhead and their anxious faces looked pale and ghostly in the lamplight.

"Sally told me she had robbed the boy's mother of something," said Mrs Bumble. "Something gold."

"Did she sell it?" asked Monks, urgently. "Where? When?"

"She died before she could tell me more."

"It's a lie!" cried Monks. "She must have said more. Tell me, or I'll tear the life out of both of you!"

"She said no more," Mrs Bumble told him, "but there was a scrap of paper – a pawnbroker's ticket. I guessed the pawnbroker had paid Sally for some trinket, and that she hoped to buy it back one day, so I went and exchanged the ticket for the goods myself."

Monks became excited. "Where are they?"

"Here," replied the woman, throwing a small leather bag on to the table as if pleased to be rid of it.

Monks pounced on it with trembling hands. Inside was a little gold locket containing two locks of hair, and a plain gold wedding ring.

"It has the name 'Agnes' engraved on the inside," said Mrs Bumble, "and a date which is within a year of Oliver's birth."

"And this is all?" said Monks.

"All," said Mrs Bumble. She looked anxious. "What are you going to do with them? Can they be used against me by the police?"

"Never!" answered Monks. "Nor me, either. Watch!"

And he pushed the table aside to reveal a trap door in the

floor. Once the door was lifted, they saw the river running underneath, swollen by the heavy rain. Monks put the locket and ring back into the bag and tied it to a heavy weight before dropping it into the foaming water.

"There!" said Monks. "It's finished. If you're wise, you'll forget me and all that's happened tonight."

Mr and Mrs Bumble were only too happy to agree. They took their money and hurried away.

Chapter Nine

Bill Sikes lifted his head from the pillow and asked what time it was. He was thin and sickly looking and there was a week's growth of beard on his face. His dog, Bulls-eye, sat beside the bed.

"Not long past seven o'clock," Nancy told him.

"Help me up," he growled, then cursed her for being clumsy, and knocked her to the floor.

Just then, Fagin arrived with the Artful Dodger and Charley.

"What's the matter here?" said Fagin, helping Nancy to her feet.

"What evil wind has blown you here?" said Sikes. "Why haven't you been before?"

"I've been away from London for a week or more," said Fagin.

"I must have some money from you tonight," Sikes told him.

"I haven't a single coin with me, my dear," replied Fagin.

"Then take Nancy back with you. She can bring my money back."

After much argument, Fagin managed to reduce the amount Sikes was demanding from five pounds to three, then he went back to his house with Nancy and the two boys.

When they arrived, Fagin sent the boys out and was just going upstairs to unlock the cupboard when he and Nancy heard a knock at the front door.

"That's the man I was expecting earlier," said Fagin. "He won't be here long, but not a word about the money, Nancy."

He went to the door and opened it. Monks stood in the doorway.

"I have good news," said Fagin.

"Tell me in private," said Monks when he saw Nancy.

"Wait here," Fagin told Nancy, then took Monks upstairs to a room.

Nancy quickly slipped off her shoes and crept up after them. She stood outside the door, holding her breath and listening to the two men talking inside. Slowly, the colour drained from her face.

When the men came out, Nancy was at the bottom of the stairs again.

"You look pale, my dear," said Fagin, after Monks had gone. "Is something wrong?"

"Only that I've been kept waiting too long for Bill's money," said Nancy, turning her face away from him.

Fagin counted out the money, with a sigh at every coin that left his hand, then the girl said a quick "Goodnight" and left him.

Out in the street, Nancy sat down on a doorstep, worried and confused. Then, instead of heading towards Sikes' lodgings, she ran wildly in the opposite direction until she was exhausted. After she had stopped crying and had calmed herself, Nancy turned and hurried back to Sikes.

At first he noticed nothing strange about her, and the next day happily spent Fagin's money on drink. But when he eventually returned home, some of Nancy's nervous excitement caught his attention.

"You look like a corpse come to life again," he said. "What is it?"

"Nothing," replied Nancy.

Sikes became suspicious, but Nancy quickly poured out his medicine with her back towards him, then gave it to him. She watched as he slowly sank into a deep sleep.

"The sleeping drug has worked at last," she murmured, standing up, "but I may still be too late."

She quickly put on her bonnet and shawl, stooped softly over the bed and kissed the robber's lips, then noiselessly hurried from the house.

Many of the shops were closing as Nancy elbowed her way through the crowded streets towards the West End of London. Her destination was a small family hotel in a quiet street near Hyde Park. The clock struck eleven as she went up the steps.

"I want to speak to Miss Rose Maylie," she told the porter.

At first the man refused, but eventually Nancy was taken to Miss Maylie's room where the young lady asked how she could help her.

"I'm about to put my life and the lives of others into your hands," said Nancy. She hesitated, then went on, "I'm the girl who dragged little Oliver back to Fagin on the night he went on an errand for Mr Brownlow."

"You!" said Rose Maylie.

"Yes, lady," replied Nancy. "I'm that wicked person who lives among thieves. They would murder me if they knew I was here to tell you what I've overheard. Do you know a man called Monks?"

"No," answered Rose.

"He knows you, and knows you're here. I heard him tell Fagin."

"But I never heard his name before," said Rose.

"Then he's using a false one, as I suspected," said Nancy. "I overheard a conversation between him and Fagin and learned that Monks had been searching for Oliver, and had seen him – purely by chance – the day Oliver got arrested. I didn't hear why Monks was looking for Oliver, but I heard him make a bargain with Fagin. He agreed to pay a large sum of money if Fagin could turn Oliver into a thief."

"But why?" asked Rose.

"I don't know. Monks saw my shadow on the wall and I had to escape quickly. But last night, he came to see Fagin again when I was there."

"What happened then?"

"I listened at the door," said Nancy, "and I heard Monks say, 'So the only evidence of the boy's identity is at the bottom of the river, and the old hag that took them from his mother is rotting in her coffin.' Then they laughed, and Monks said that he had all Oliver's money safely now but was afraid the boy might find out about his father's will or the identity of his parents. 'If that happens, Fagin,' he said, 'I shall be forced to kill my young brother, Oliver.'"

"His brother!" exclaimed Rose.

"Those were his words. And then he said what a strange coincidence it was that Oliver should come into your hands, and that you would give thousands of pounds to know who Oliver really was," Nancy looked round, nervously. "But it's late, I must get back."

"Back!" said Rose. "I can find you a safe place and you can tell your story – "

"No!" said Nancy. "There's a man, the most desperate of them all, and I can't leave him, not now. I cannot be the cause of his death."

"But how can I find you?" pleaded Rose. "This mystery must be investigated further, for Oliver's sake."

"I'll tell you, but you must promise to keep it a secret," said Nancy.

"I promise," the other girl replied.

"Every Sunday, after midnight, I will walk on London Bridge, if I'm still alive," said Nancy. "Now I must go. God bless you, lady."

Rose passed a sleepless night, trying to decide what was the best thing to do. She was still puzzling about it in the morning when Oliver burst into her room. He had been walking in the streets with one of the servants for a bodyguard, but now he could hardly contain his excitement.

"I've seen Mr Brownlow!" he cried. "He was going into a house. Here, I've got the address!"

"Then we must go there at once," said Rose.

Within minutes they were on their way in a coach.

Rose left Oliver outside whilst she went into the house to see the old gentleman. He was sitting in his study.

"You once showed kindness to a dear friend of mine," said Rose, "and I'm sure you'll be interested to hear news of him."

"Indeed?" said Mr Brownlow. "May I ask his name?"

"Oliver Twist," replied Rose.

The astonished Mr Brownlow was speechless for several moments, then he said, "I once thought the boy to be a liar and a thief, but I've been abroad and have discovered certain things which make me doubt that now. Tell me what you know of him."

Rose told Oliver's story, ending it by saying that the boy's greatest sadness had been not finding Mr Brownlow. "He's out in the coach," she told the old gentleman, "waiting to see you."

Mr Brownlow rushed outside, and in a minute returned with Oliver. Mrs Bedwin was sent for immediately and could not believe her eyes.

"God be good to me!" she cried, hugging Oliver. "My little boy!"

"My dear old nurse!" sobbed Oliver.

Whilst they hugged and kissed, Rose asked Mr Brownlow if they could go into another room. She had decided to trust him with Nancy's secrets.

On that same evening, two people who had once helped to make Oliver's life a misery were in London, looking for cheap lodgings for the night. They had stumbled on the Three Cripples Inn and were tucking into a supper of cold meat and beer. Noah Claypole and Charlotte had grown tired of the undertaking business and had robbed old Mr Sowerberry of his money before coming to the city. Now, as Noah boasted about how clever they had been, and what other profitable crimes they might try their hands at, he was alarmed to discover that every word had been overheard by a stranger. An old, evil-looking man with a tangled beard. The man introduced himself. It was Fagin.

"Don't be alarmed, my dears," said Fagin. "I can help you."

He had been on the look-out for a new helper or two, for

only that week the Dodger – his best man! – had been arrested for pick-pocketing and sent to prison.

Now he was about to get two new lodgers. Noah and Charlotte.

Chapter Ten

It was Sunday night and the church clock struck eleven.

"An hour before midnight," said Bill Sikes, looking out into the darkness. "A good night for business."

Fagin was with him and agreed. "A pity there's no job to be done."

Nancy was putting on her bonnet when Sikes noticed her.

"Where are you going at this time of night?" he wanted to know.

"Not far," she said.

"What kind of answer is that? Sit down!"

"No!" Nancy stamped her foot and turned to Fagin. "Tell him to let me go, Fagin!"

"Another word, and I'll set the dog on you!" shouted Sikes. He pulled the bonnet from her head and threw it across the room.

"Bill let me go! You don't know what you're doing!"

Sikes seized her by the arm and she struggled wildly. "The girl's mad!" he cried.

"Perhaps she's got a fever," said Fagin, watching her closely.

But later, as he went home, Fagin grew suspicious. Why had the girl been so desperate to go out at that particular hour? Did she have a new friend whom she hoped could help her escape from Sikes and his brutal ways? But Sikes would never let her go. Unless ...

Fagin had an idea. If he could find out who Nancy's new friend was, then he could threaten to tell Bill. Then Nancy would be in his power! She would do anything to stop Sikes finding out. Even … poison him? That would please Fagin. Sikes had grown dangerous. He knew enough about Fagin's crimes to get the old man hanged.

The next day, Fagin told Noah he had a job for him.

The following Sunday night, two figures moved across London Bridge. A mist hung over the river, and the blackened, smoke-stained warehouses on either side rose high among the dense mass of smaller buildings.

Noah was careful to keep in the shadows as he watched the girl. Then a church clock chimed midnight and a carriage came to a stop at one end of the bridge. A man and a woman got out and Nancy hurried towards them. She took them down some steps to a stone wharf, and Noah padded silently after them. Moments later, he heard them speaking.

"I couldn't come last Sunday," Nancy said. "They kept me in. And now I am so frightened I can hardly stand. Horrible thoughts of death have been with me all day."

"Imagination," said Mr Brownlow, soothing her, "Now, tell us about Mr Monks. How can we get him?"

"But, Fagin and the others – " began Nancy.

"They will never know how we found out about Monks," Mr Brownlow assured her.

Satisfied, Nancy told them about the Three Cripples Inn and when they would be most likely to find Monks there. She began to describe him.

"High on his throat," she said, "there's – "

"A bright red mark, like a burn!" cried Mr Brownlow.

"Yes!" said Nancy. "Do you know him?"

"I think I do. Now, you've been most helpful. What can we do for you in return?"

"Nothing, sir," replied Nancy. "I'm chained to my old life, I cannot leave it. And now I must go home."

With that, she ran back up the steps and away into the night. Soon after, Mr Brownlow and Rose returned to their carriage.

By then, the astonished Noah was already running towards Fagin's house as fast as his legs would carry him.

Noah had to tell his story twice. Once to Fagin, and then

again at dawn when Bill Sikes arrived at the house. Sikes came with a bundle of stolen goods, and Fagin dragged Noah from his sleep to repeat what he'd heard.

Sikes listened with a growing rage, then rushed from the room before Fagin could stop him.

"Bill!" Fagin shouted after him. "Don't be too violent with her!"

Sikes made no reply. He ran headlong back to his house, opening the door softly and creeping upstairs where Nancy was sleeping.

"Get up!" he shouted.

"Bill!" she said, waking. At first she looked pleased to see him, but then she saw the expression on his face and her blood ran cold through her veins. "What have I done?"

"You know what you've done, you she-devil!"

Sikes took a pistol from his pocket and was about to fire it when he realised the sound might be heard. Instead, he beat it twice against her head and face. Then the murderer staggered to a corner of the room, seized a heavy club and struck her down.

Sikes sat looking at the body, afraid to move. It was morning, and the sun had burst upon the crowded city. It shone into that room, making the scene even more ghastly in its brilliant light. At last, he threw a rug over the body and fled from the building, his dog running behind him.

'I have to get out of London,' he thought. 'It's too dangerous to stay here.'

So he made for the country. But when darkness fell, the ghost of Nancy haunted him. He could hear her cry in every low moan of the wind, saw her figure in every shadow. He found a field to sleep in, but visions of her dead staring eyes kept him awake until morning.

Sikes found no peace. Each day was spent constantly looking over his shoulder, and at night Nancy came between him and his sleep. At last, he decided to go back to London and take his chances.

"At least there'll be someone to talk to," he said to himself, "and places to hide." Then he looked at Bulls-eye. "If anything can give me away, it's you. Once they see you, they'll know where to find me."

He decided to drown the animal, and found a heavy stone which he tied to his handkerchief. But the dog seemed to sense what was about to happen and ran away. Sikes whistled again and again, but the animal kept out of sight. At last, Sikes set off for London.

Chapter Eleven

Mr Brownlow had finally got his man. Monks was seen coming from the Three Cripples Inn by the old gentleman and one of his servants, and was quickly bundled into a carriage and brought to Mr Brownlow's house.

"Fraud and robbery," Mr Brownlow told him. "Those are the charges I can have brought against you."

"Fine treatment from my father's oldest friend!" protested Monks, who had been surprised to be kidnapped in the street by a familiar face. A face he hoped never to see again.

"It's because I was his friend that I'll treat you gently now, Mr Edward Leeford," replied Mr Brownlow, using Monks' real name.

"What do you want with me?"

"You have a brother – "

"I do not have a brother!" said Monks. "I was an only child."

"Your father was forced into an unhappy marriage," Mr Brownlow went on smoothly, "and you were born. But your parents separated and your mother went to live abroad, taking you with her. Ten years later, your father fell in love with a beautiful young girl and planned to marry her. But then a rich relation of his died and left him a lot of money. Your father had to travel to Rome to claim it, but after arriving there became ill and died. You and your mother heard about this and rushed to his deathbed. As he had made no will, all the relation's money came to you and her."

Monks listened intently but said nothing.

"Before your father went to Rome," Mr Brownlow went on, "he came to see me. Ah! I see you didn't know that! He brought me a portrait of the girl he wanted to marry. Later, when I heard of your father's death, I went to look for the girl but she and her family had left the address a week earlier, and nobody knew where they'd gone."

Monks breathed easier and smiled.

Mr Brownlow moved his chair closer to the other man. "But when, by happy chance, your brother came to my notice and I was able to rescue him from a life of villainy – "

"What!" cried Monks.

"Oh yes, he was taken from the court by me. And then I noticed his likeness to the girl in the portrait, and I saw the glimpse of an old friend in his face. But I need not tell you he was snatched away before I discovered his history."

"You – you can't prove anything," stammered Monks.

"We shall see. I lost the boy and could not find him. Your mother being dead, I knew that you alone could solve the mystery. I'd heard that you'd gone to the West Indies so I travelled there, only to discover that you had returned to London. But now I've found you."

"Fraud and robbery are high-sounding words," said Monks. "Brother! You don't even know whether the pair had a child."

"I didn't know it, but now I do. In the last fortnight I learned that you have a brother, and that you knew it too. And your father left a will that your mother destroyed. It mentioned a boy that would be born later – a boy you later tried to find, going to the town where he was born. And when you found proof of his birth, you destroyed it – a gold locket and a wedding ring. 'The only evidence of the boy's identity is at the bottom of the river, and the old hag that took them from his mother is rotting in her coffin.'"

Monks was shocked into silence by his own words, overwhelmed by how much the other man knew.

"Yes, shadows on the wall have caught your whispers," said Mr Brownlow. "But now murder has been done – "

"I know nothing of murder!" cried Monks.

"It **was** done because of you and your secrets. Now, will you sign a confession before witnesses? Tell the whole story?"

Monks knew he was beaten. "If you insist upon it," he replied.

"And you must carry out your father's wishes for your brother, and give Oliver what is really his. Then you can go where you please. Somewhere in the world where we may never meet again."

While Monks was pacing up and down, torn by fear on one hand, and hatred on the other, the door was opened and a servant came in.

"The murderer will be taken tonight," the man said. "His dog has been found near one of his old haunts, and there's little doubt that Sikes will be there soon, if he isn't already."

"And Fagin?" said Mr Brownlow.

"The police are sure of him. He can't escape."

Mr Brownlow turned to Monks. "Well, have you made up your mind?"

"Yes," said Monks. "If it will all stay a secret, I agree."

In Jacob's Island, down by the river Thames, the warehouses were roofless and empty, the walls were crumbling down, and where there were once windows now there were only black holes. Only the poorest people and criminals lived in this, the dirtiest, roughest part of London.

In the upper room of a ruin of a house, three men sat talking.

"When was Fagin taken?" asked Toby Crackit.

"The police came at dinner-time," replied a man called Chitling. "Charley Bates and I escaped up the wash-house chimney. Charley will be here soon."

"Fagin will hang," said the third man, who was called Kags.

A pattering noise came on the stairs and seconds later,

Bulls-eye, Sikes' dog bounded into the room.

"What's the meaning of this?" gasped Toby. "I … I hope Sikes isn't coming here!"

His hopes were in vain. An hour later, the white-faced Sikes appeared at the door. He glared at the dog when he saw him.

"How did he get here?"

Before anyone could answer, there were more footsteps and Charley Bates arrived. He saw Sikes and immediately began to back away.

"Charley," said Sikes, putting out a hand.

"Don't come near me!" cried the boy, horror in his eyes. "Murderer! If the police come, I'll give you to them! Help! Help!"

There were lights appearing outside, and the shouts of many voices. Then somebody was pounding the locked outside door.

"Help!" shrieked Charley. "Sikes is up here!"

Sikes ran to the window and looked down. He shook his fist at the crowd below. "Do your worst. I'll cheat you yet!" he shouted at them. Then he turned to the others in the room. "Get me a rope, or I'll do three more murders!"

They quickly found one and, minutes later, Sikes appeared on the roof. The shouts from the crowd swelled to one huge cry as they saw him.

"They have him now!" cried a man on the nearest bridge.

Sikes tied one end of the rope around a chimney and the other into a noose, ready to let himself down to safety, behind the house. But at the very instant he put the loop over his head to slip it under his armpits, he looked over his shoulder and let out a cry of terror.

"Nancy's eyes!" he screamed. "The eyes again!"

Staggering, as if struck by lightning, Sikes lost his balance and fell. The noose was at his neck and it tightened with a deadly jerk as he dropped over the edge of the roof.

The murderer was dead, his body swinging lifeless against the wall.

Bulls-eye, who had climbed out on to the roof, jumped

towards Sikes' shoulders with a dismal howl. Missing its aim, the dog fell down to its death.

Chapter Twelve

Two days after Sikes died, Oliver was taken back to the town where he was born. Mrs Maylie and Rose travelled with him, and Mr Brownlow was to follow later. He had told Oliver some of his history, but much of it was still a mystery.

That evening, after supper at the town's largest hotel, Mr Brownlow arrived with Monks. Oliver saw him and gasped.

"That's the man who I saw with Fagin!" he cried.

"I know. Oliver, this is your half-brother. And this," Mr Brownlow said, turning to Monks, "is your half-brother, Oliver, the son of your father and of poor Agnes Fleming, who died when Oliver was born. Now, tell the boy everything."

Monks stared at the boy with hatred in his eyes.

"Amongst my father's papers when he died, was a letter to the girl, Agnes, and a will. The letter asked her not to curse his memory or think too badly of him if he should die before they could be married. He reminded her of the day he'd given her the little locket, and ring with her name engraved on it."

"And the will!" said Mr Brownlow, as Oliver's eyes filled with tears.

Monks was silent.

"In the will," said Mr Brownlow, "your father spoke of the misery of his marriage and the wicked son who had been taught to hate him. He left you and your mother an income of £800 a year, and the rest of his property went to Agnes Fleming and their child, if it were born alive – and if the child never did anything wrong or unkind or criminal."

Monks spoke at last. "My mother burnt the will and never sent the letter. Later, she gave it to me and told me about the will, and that Agnes had given birth to a boy. I swore to her when she was dying that I would find the boy."

"And the locket and the ring?"

"I bought them from the man and woman I told you of, who stole them from the nurse. You know what happened to them."

Mr Brownlow nodded to a servant who went out and came back into the room moments later with Mr Bumble and his wife.

"Oliver!" cried Mr Bumble. "Is it really you? You know how I always loved you as if you were my own."

"Do you know this man?" Mr Brownlow asked him, pointing to Monks.

"No!" said Mr Bumble.

"No!" echoed his wife.

"He has confessed," Mr Brownlow told them. "We know everything about the locket and the ring."

"If this man has been coward enough to confess all," said Mrs Bumble, "then I have nothing more to say."

"I – I hope this unfortunate matter will not mean I lose my position at the workhouse –" began Mr Bumble, looking rueful.

"Indeed it will," replied Mr Brownlow. "I'll see neither of you are employed in a position of trust ever again. Now, go!"

When they had been removed from the room, Mr Brownlow turned to Rose, "There is just one more thing," he said, taking her hand. "The father of poor Agnes had two daughters. Monks, tell us what you know of the other one, who was only a child when Oliver was born."

"Her father died in a strange place and she was taken in by a poor family, who brought her up," said Monks. "But a lady saw the child, took pity on her and gave her a home."

"When did you last see Agnes' sister?" asked Mr Brownlow.

"Two or three years ago, then again recently."

"Do you see her now?"

"Yes," said Monks. "She's leaning on your arm."

Rose almost fainted, but Oliver threw his arms around her neck.

"My mother's sister!" he cried, joyfully. "But I can never call you aunt. You will always be my own dear sister!"

Fagin sat alone in the condemned man's cell. It was cold and dark, and seemed full of other ghosts who had been there before him.

The night before he was due to be hanged, Mr Brownlow and Oliver came to see him.

"You have some papers, given to you by a man called Monks," said Mr Brownlow.

"It's a lie!" said Fagin.

"Sikes is dead and Monks has confessed everything, Fagin," Mr Brownlow told him. "What have you to lose by telling us?"

Fagin beckoned to Oliver. "Come here," he said, and took the boy's hand. "The letter is in a hole in the chimney of my top front-room. But now you must help me." He pushed Oliver towards the cell door, madness in the old man's eyes. "Say I've gone to sleep – they'll believe you. Take me with you. If I tremble as we pass the gallows, don't worry, but hurry on. Now, now!"

The jailers laid hands on Fagin and pulled him away from Oliver. The old man struggled and sent up a terrible cry. It echoed around them and was still in Oliver's ears when he and Mr Brownlow finally got outside.

Now Oliver's life of misery and hardship was behind him. Mr Brownlow adopted him, and they went to live in the same village as Rose and Mrs Maylie. There were many happy days ahead for all of them.

Within the old village church there now stands a white marble stone, bearing the word 'AGNES'. It stands in memory of a mother of a boy.

A boy called Oliver Twist.